D1221311

For Ella and Riley

Published by The Ella Riley Group,
86-90 Paul Street, London, EC2A 4NE

www.davinahamilton.com

© The Ella Riley Group 2020

All rights reserved. Without limiting the rights under copyright reserved above,
no part of this publication may be reproduced, stored in or introduced into
a retrieval system, or transmitted in any form or by any means
(electronic, mechanical, photocopying, recording or otherwise),
without the prior written permission of both the copyright owner
and the above publisher of the book.

A catalogue record of this book is available from the British Library.

ISBN: 9780995700574

Printed in China

ELLA HAS A PLAN

Words by Davina Hamilton

Illustration by Elena Reinoso

Ella was thinking, her mind was in gear
(Although the hairdryer was all she could hear!)
But still, there was only one thing on her mind:
How could she get Taye and Jade to be kind?

They were her cousins and they'd soon be here,
With lots of the family from far and near.
Today was the day when they'd all celebrate
At Mummy's big party, and it would be great!

But Ella was worried about Taye and Jade,
They'd argue and bicker whenever they played!
So all that was whizzing through poor Ella's mind
Was finding a way to teach them to be kind.

"Mummy?" said Ella. "When everyone's here
I know we'll have fun – but I just have one fear:
I think Taye and Jade might fall out when we play,
And that would upset me and spoil your big day!"

"You know," Mummy said, "this sounds just like a story
About Grandad Glen and his sister, Aunt Glory.
When they were little, they often fell out,
And always found something to argue about!"

"But their clever daddy – your Great Grandad Frank,
Came up with an idea to play a great prank.
His trick taught his kids to be kind to each other
And always play nicely as sister and brother."

"Mummy?" said Ella. "What was the great prank?"
Mummy replied, "Ask your Great Grandad Frank.
When he gets here later, he'll tell you the story
About how he tricked Grandad Glen and Aunt Glory!"

"But I'll tell you this," Mummy said with a smile,
"When Taye and Jade get here in just a short while,
You'll sort any quarrels, I know that you can.
You're such a smart girl, you'll come up with a plan."

Choose
TO BE
HAPPY

Soon Mummy's party was coming alive,
As all of the family began to arrive!
Chef Uncle Ted brought all of the food:
Some roasted, some fried, and some barbecued!

As all the family was milling about,
Ella remembered she had to find out:
The mystery tale of how Great Grandad Frank
Had stopped his kids quarrelling with a great prank.

Ella found Great Grandad Frank on the chair.
She gave him a hug, as she stroked his grey hair.
Then she asked him: "Can you tell me the story
Of how you once tricked Grandad Glen and Aunt Glory?"

"Woiii!" he exclaimed, as he chuckled out loud.
"Now that is a story that makes me feel proud!
I'll tell you, but first, please do something for me:
Ask Uncle Ted to bring me some mint tea."

"No problem, I'll do that for you," Ella said.
So she went in the kitchen and asked Uncle Ted.
"Ok," he replied, as he prepped Mummy's cake.
And then he exclaimed: "This took ages to make!"

Ella looked up at the big cake and said:
"How did you make it all blue, Uncle Ted?"
"Ah," he replied, "that was easy to do.
I used blue food colouring to make it all blue."

"Wow," Ella said. "Now that's pretty cool.
The cake looks so tasty it's making me drool!"
Uncle Ted laughed. "I hope it will be!
Now go and have fun, I'll bring the mint tea."

Ella went back to her Great Grandad Frank.
By now she was bursting to hear of his prank!
"Now," Ella said, "Can I *please* hear the story
Of how you once tricked Grandad Glen and Aunt Glory?"

"Well," he began, "those dear children of mine,
I wanted them both to just get along fine.
But all of the time they would quarrel and fight.
They'd start in the morning, right through to the night!"

"They'd fuss and they'd squabble; they'd huff and they'd puff,
Until I decided that I'd had enough!
I said to myself, you can sort this out, man.
You just need to think and come up with a plan!"

"Ooh!" Ella said, smiling from ear to ear.
"This is the part I've been bursting to hear!"
Then, from behind her, she heard someone yelp.
It was little Riley who said, "I need help!"

Ella jumped swiftly and said to her brother:
"Is it Taye and Jade arguing with each other?"
"Yes," Riley cried. "They're both starting to shout.
And nobody knows how to sort them both out!"

Great Grandad Frank started shaking his head.
He took Ella's hand and then smiled as he said:
"You go and sort them, I know that you can.
You're clever like me – you'll come up with a plan!"

Ella found all of her cousins upstairs.
Both Taye and Jade were exchanging mean glares!
"What's going on?" Ella said, with a frown.
"It's Jade!" Taye exclaimed. "She keeps putting me down!"

"I'm not!" bellowed Jade. "Taye's the one being mean!
He said my dance was the worst thing he'd seen!"
"It was!" Taye said loudly. "Jade really can't dance!"
"I can!" Jade exclaimed. "Taye won't give me a chance!

"When I was dancing, Taye started to sing.
And his awful voice really messed up my swing!"
"You see!" Taye exclaimed. "Jade is silly and mean!"
"I'm not!" Jade yelled back. "Taye's the silly old bean!"

Ella stood quietly, then shook her head.
She looked at her quarrelling cousins and said:
"Come on, you two, this just isn't right –
You're both great performers, there's no need to fight."

"Jade, you can dance. And Taye, you can sing!"
Riley agreed: "They can be anything!"
"Exactly!" said Ella. "So it's such a shame
That both of you argue – when you're quite the same!"

Taye and Jade couldn't believe what they'd heard.
Jade looked at Ella and said: "That's absurd!
I'm nothing like Taye, and he's nothing like me!"
"Exactly!" said Taye. "That's easy to see!"

Ella was fed up; she let out a huff.
She needed a plan because she'd had enough!
Her mind started whizzing, but what could she do?
Her quarrelling cousins were making her blue...

Right then it happened – a great idea came:
An idea to show them that they are the same.
Yes, Ella thought – I can fix this, I can.
I've just come up with the most brilliant plan!

Ella went downstairs and found Uncle Ted.
She smiled a wide smile, as she quietly said:
"I need you to help me sort out Jade and Taye."
So Uncle Ted heard what his niece had to say.

When she was done, Uncle Ted was wide-eyed.
"Ella, you're truly amazing!" he cried.
"You need me to help you? My dear, sure I can!
 You really have thought up a brilliant plan!"

Ella called all of her cousins downstairs.
She asked them to sit on the dining room chairs.
Uncle Ted came in with cups on a tray
And said to them all: "Here's a game we can play…"

"I've made a drink full of fresh fruits, you see –
I'd like you to guess what those nice fruits could be.
But when you start drinking, you must close your eyes,
And then you'll be in for an extra surprise!"

They all closed their eyes; they all got a drink;
They all took a sip, and then started to think.
"I taste pineapple," big cousin Joe uttered.
"I can taste mango," Nathaniel then muttered.

Riley said loudly: "I think I taste lime.
Whenever I sip, I can taste it each time!"
All of the children continued to drink,
But both Taye and Jade were unsure what to think.

"I can't taste any of those," Jade called out.
"I have no idea what you're all on about!"
"Exactly!" said Taye. "When I sip every time,
I can't taste pineapple, or mango, or lime!"

Uncle Ted chuckled, "You're all doing great.
But now's the big moment – I'm sure you can't wait!
So let's move along with no further delay.
Please open your eyes, as the fun's on its way!"

All of the children then opened their eyes.
Joe said excitedly: "What's the surprise?"
Uncle Ted smiled as he said: "You tell me.
Look at each other, and then you will see."

Ella then giggled – she felt so amused.
"Why are you laughing?" Jade asked, all confused.
"Yeah, what's so funny?" Taye wanted a clue.
And then they all saw it…

Their tongues were bright BLUE!

Jade looked at Taye and said: "Your tongue is blue!"
Taye looked at Jade and said: "Yours is blue, too!"
Ella then said to them: "This was my game
To show both of you that you are quite the same!"

"Yes, you have differences – that's a good thing.
Jade, you can dance, and Taye, you can sing.
But in lots of ways, you are similar too –
Especially now that your tongues are bright blue!"

They all shrieked with laughter at Ella's great trick;
Both Taye and Jade thought it was pretty slick!
"You got us!" Jade chuckled; and Taye said, "Oh man!
I have to admit, this was such a cool plan!"

Ella felt all warm and fuzzy inside.
Her idea had worked – she was beaming with pride!
Her cousins were no longer angry or sad,
Instead they were laughing and Ella was glad.

Later that night, as the music was playing,
All of the family was dancing and swaying.
Taye sang out loudly and Jade showed her moves;
And Uncle Baz played some fantastic jazz grooves!

The party continued well into the night,
And Ella was thrilled at the wonderful sight.
Of all of her family having such fun,
Until late at night when the party was done.

Later, when Mummy put Ella to bed,
She cuddled her doll and then smiled as she said:
"I like solving problems – I know that I can,
As long as I always come up with a plan."

Mummy said softly, "My girl is so smart –
And not only that, you've got such a kind heart.
I'm proud of the way that you helped Jade and Taye.
But now get some sleep – you've sure had a long day!"

When Mummy left, Ella lay in her bed,
And then a thought suddenly popped in her head:
Great Grandad Frank didn't tell her the story
About how he tricked Grandad Glen and Aunt Glory!

Ella then thought about her clever prank:
Had she played the same trick as Great Grandad Frank?
She said to herself: "Now I need a new plan:
To find out *that* story as soon as I can!"

ELLA
HAS A PLAN

Words by Davina Hamilton

Illustration by Elena Reinoso

Daddy   Ella   Riley   Mummy

Uncle Baz   Nathaniel   Taye   Aunty Kay

Uncle Dan   Jade   Aunty Sheriece

Joe

Aunty Sophie

Uncle Ted

Young Glen   Young Glory

Great Grandad Frank

CAN YOU COME UP WITH A PLAN?
What do you think Great Grandad Frank's prank was?
Why not come up with your own plan for him and
write your own story? Have fun!